KT-131-818

FUNNYBONES

Other books by Allan Ahlberg

A BIT MORE BERT

THE ADVENTURES OF BERT

The FAST FOX, SLOW DOG series (illus. André Amstutz)

FUNNYBONES: THE BLACK CAT (illus. André Amstutz)

The HAPPY FAMILIES series (illus. various)

THE LITTLE CAT BABY

Other books by Janet and Allan Ahlberg

BURGLAR BILL

BYE BYE BABY

THE CLOTHES HORSE AND OTHER STORIES

COPS AND ROBBERS

EACH PEACH PEAR PLUM

FUNNYBONES

IT WAS A DARK AND STORMY NIGHT

JEREMIAH IN THE DARK WOODS

THE JOLLY CHRISTMAS POSTMAN

THE JOLLY POSTMAN

THE JOLLY POCKET POSTMAN

STARTING SCHOOL

The Pet Shop

ALLAN AHLBERG • ANDRÉ AMSTUTZ

PUFFIN

In a dark dark – Woof! – street
there is a dark dark – Woof! – house.
Behind the dark dark – Woof! – house
there is a dark dark – Woof! – garden.
In the dark dark – Woof! – garden
there is a very dark dark –
Woof! – hole
WOOF!
woof!
Woof!
Woof!
Woof!
WOOF!

. . . and a little noisy dog – Woof!

One night, the big skeleton
and the little skeleton
go into the garden.
"I'm fed up with this dog,"
says the little skeleton.
"Me too," says the big skeleton.
"All he does is dig holes – and bark."
"Woof!" barks the dog.

"I know," says the little skeleton,
"let's go to the pet shop –
and swap him."
"Good idea!" the big skeleton says.
"Howl!" howls the dog.

£1
A FOOT
Moo!
Squeak!
Grunt!
CREAKO
for creaky bones

So off they – Woof! – go,
out of the dark dark garden,
down the dark dark street
and into the dark dark – Miaow! –
– Squeak! – Grunt! – pet shop.
The big skeleton and the little skeleton
swap the dog – Woof! – skeleton

. . . for a goldfish.

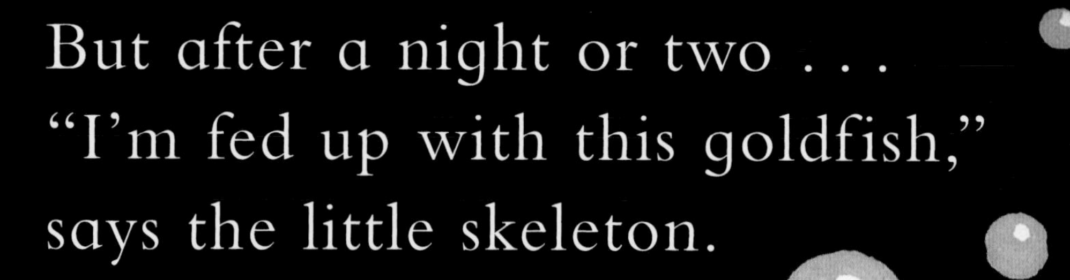

But after a night or two . . .
"I'm fed up with this goldfish,"
says the little skeleton.

"Me too," says the big skeleton.
"All it does is blow bubbles –
and swim."

So off they go again,
out of the dark dark house,
down the dark dark street
and back to the dark dark – Miaow! –
– Snort! – Croak! – pet shop.
The big skeleton and the little skeleton
swap the goldfish – Bubble, bubble! – skeleton
. . . for a parrot.

Four eyes!
Smelly socks!
BANDY LEGS!
Bean pole!
Baldy!
Fatty belly!

But after another night or two . . .
"I'm fed up with this parrot,"
says the little skeleton.
"Me too," says the big skeleton.
"All he does is shout rude names."
"Big bum!" shouts the parrot.

So off they go again,
back to the dark dark – Miaow! –
– Big bum! – pet shop.
The big skeleton and the little skeleton
swap the parrot skeleton
Long nose!
Pig face!

. . . for a hippopotamus.
But the hippopotamus
is no good either.
All he does . . .

. . . is fill the room!

So – Wobble, wobble! –
back they go again
and swap the hippopotamus
. . . for a rabbit.
Big ears!

And after a night or two . . .
"I love this rabbit,"
says the little skeleton.
"Me too," says the big skeleton.
"He's not big,
he's not cheeky
and he doesn't blow bubbles."

The only trouble is – *he* is not a *he*.

So after a few more nights . . .
"I'm fed up with these rabbits,"
says the little skeleton.
"And these!" the big skeleton says.

Back they go to the pet shop.
"And I'm fed up with this
– Miaow! – Moo! – Baa! –
pet shop as well!"
says the little skeleton.

The pet-shop skeleton
puts the rabbits in a hutch.
"Cheer up!" he says.
"I've got just the thing for you."

He gives them a big box
with little holes in it.
"But don't open it until
you get home."

After that the big skeleton
and the little skeleton
leave the dark dark –
Miaow! – pet shop, and
hurry down the dark dark street
to the dark dark house
. . . and the dark dark cellar.

They put the box on the table.
"I wonder what it is,"
says the little skeleton.
"Me too," says the big skeleton.
. . . "WOOF!" barks the box.
Woof!

The End

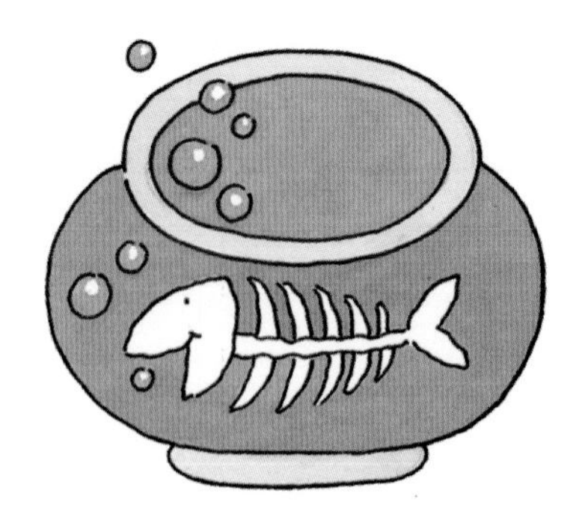

PUFFIN BOOKS

UK | USA | Canada | Ireland | Australia
India | New Zealand | South Africa

Puffin Books is part of the Penguin Random House group of companies
whose addresses can be found at global.penguinrandomhouse.com.

www.penguin.co.uk www.puffin.co.uk www.ladybird.co.uk

First published by William Heinemann Ltd 1990
First published in Puffin Books 2004
This edition published 2018

001

Printed in China
A CIP catalogue record for this book is available from the British Library

ISBN: 978–0–241–37763–5

All correspondence to:
Puffin Books, Penguin Random House Children's
80 Strand, London WC2R 0RL